Bing & Bong

Bing and Bong were heading for a new adventure on the Tiny Planet of Self. They were travelling in space on their fluffy sofa.

The flockers on the Tiny Planet of Self like to play a game called 'Header Gongball' and Bing and Bong wanted to learn to play.

The polite flockers on the Tiny Planet of Self were very friendly. They were delighted when Bing and Bong asked if they could play the game with them.

Bong squeaked with excitement.

The game looked like so much fun.

The flockers explained how to play. You had to hit the other team's gong with the ball to score a point. You could only use your head, not your hands, which was just as well because,

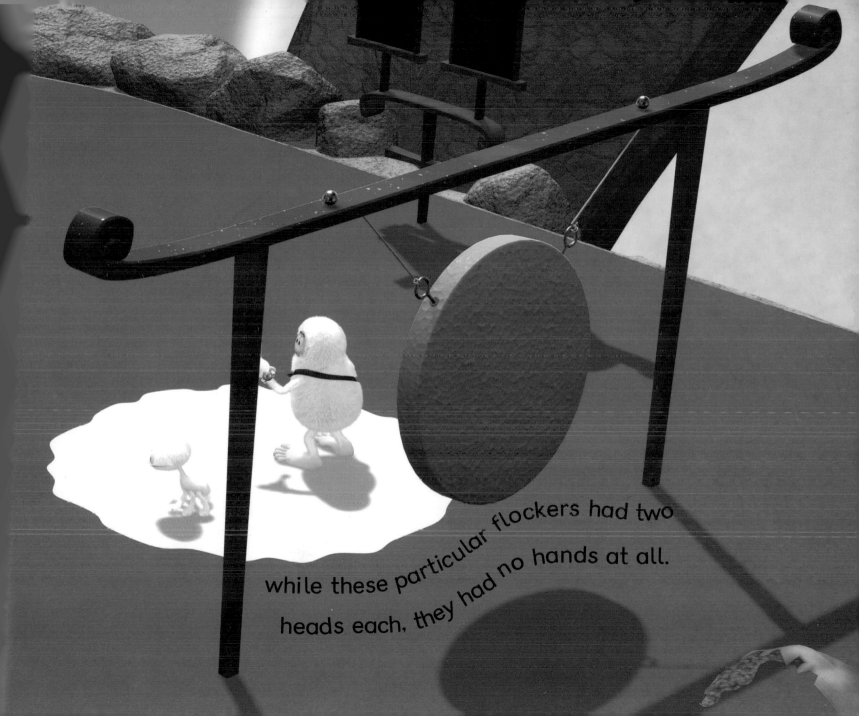

while these particular flockers had two heads each, they had no hands at all.

The flockers headed the ball towards Bing and Bong's gong. Bing jumped to try to stop it, but couldn't quite reach. The ball hit the gong, scoring a point for the flockers. Bing thought that missing the ball was rather funny and giggled. Bong didn't think it was funny.

Bong wanted to win.

The game started again and Bing tried very hard to reach the ball,

But the ball bounced off Bing's head and hit the gong.
Bong wasn't very happy. Bong wasn't going to let
the flockers win! Bong jumped to head every ball.
Then Bong scored, cheering, whooping and bouncing
up in the air to celebrate.

The polite flockers
were not used
to this sort of
behaviour.

The game restarted.
The ball went back and
forth between the flockers
and Bing and Bong until
Bing and Bong jumped at the

same time and bumped heads.
They landed in a heap on the ground.
The ball hit their gong. The flockers had
won. This made Bong feel very grumpy.
Bong didn't like losing
— not one little bit!

After a game, the flockers always bowed gracefully. The flockers bowed to Bing. Bing bowed to the flockers. The flockers bowed to Bong. Bong didn't bow back. He was not very happy about losing the game.

He wasn't being a good sport.

Even though Bong wasn't being a sport, the flockers invited Bing and Bong to play another game. Bong wasn't going to lose again! Bong jumped to head every ball and wouldn't let Bing join in the game. Bing didn't like the way Bong was acting and decided to

read a favourite comic instead.

Bong jumped up and down to head the ball and eventually scored. The flockers looked puzzled by the strange victory dance Bong performed after scoring. A few moments later, Bong scored again and the flockers collided, just as Bing and Bong had done in the first game. Bong thought this was funny and laughed out loud. The flockers did not like being laughed at.

Laughing at people was not a sporting thing to do.

The flockers didn't want to play with Bong so they hopped over to read the comic with Bing.

It didn't take Bong long to realise that playing Gongball on your own wasn't much fun.

With no one to share the excitement, no team mate to play with and no team to play against, it wasn't a proper game.

The others seemed to be having much more fun reading the comic. Bong joined in with them. After a while, Bing and the flockers started another Gongball game.

Bong asked to join in but the flockers shook their heads. The flockers didn't want to play with Bong any more. Bing felt sorry for poor Bong. Bing explained to the flockers that Bong hadn't meant to behave badly. Bong had just been too excited about playing the new game. The flockers agreed to let Bong play.

Bong jumped for joy.

This game was the most exciting of all. This time Bong and the blue flocker played against Bing and the yellow flocker. The ball was headed back and forth quickly. Bong was getting good at

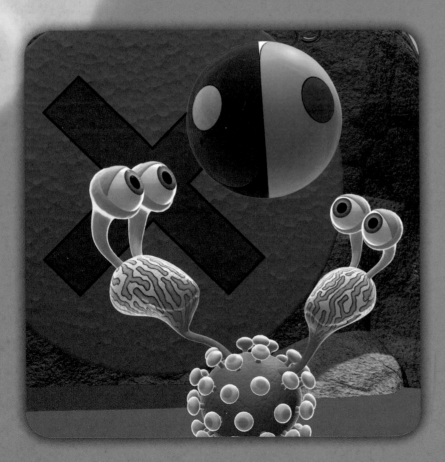

this game! Bong's team mate was very impressed. Who was going to win? Bong's flocker jumped to head the ball, but missed. The ball struck the gong. Bing's team had won. Bing hardly dared to look...

…was Bong going to be a sport?

Bong looked up and smiled. This game had been the most fun of all. Bong's team had lost, but Bong now knew that playing was fun even if you didn't win. Bong bowed to his partner and both bowed to Bing and the other flocker.

Bing felt very proud of Bong.

Just then the alarm on Bong's wristwatch sounded. It was time for them to make their way back to their sofa for the journey home.